SUPER TURBO

SAVES THE DAY!

By Lee Kirby
Illustrated by George O'Connor

LITTLE SIMON

New York   London   Toronto   Sydney   New Delhi

LITTLE SIMON

An imprint of Simon & Schuster Children's Publishing Division • 1230 Avenue of the Americas, New York, New York 10020 • First Little Simon paperback edition December 2016 • Copyright © 2016 by Simon & Schuster, Inc. All rights reserved, including the right of reproduction in whole or in part in any form. LITTLE SIMON is a registered trademark of Simon & Schuster, Inc., and associated colophon is a trademark of Simon & Schuster, Inc. For information about special discounts for bulk purchases, please contact Simon & Schuster Special Sales at 1-866-506-1949 or business@simonandschuster.com. The Simon & Schuster Speakers Bureau can bring authors to your live event. For more information or to book an event contact the Simon & Schuster Speakers Bureau at 1-866-248-3049 or visit our website at www.simonspeakers.com. Designed by Jay Colvin. The text of this book was set in Little Simon Gazette.

Manufactured in the United States of America 0319 MTN 10 9 8 7 6 5

Cataloging-in-Publication Data for this title is available from the Library of Congress.

ISBN 978-1-4814-8885-3 (hc)

ISBN 978-1-4814-8884-6 (pbk)

ISBN 978-1-4814-8886-0 (eBook)

CONTENTS

1

ALL QUIET IN CLASSROOM C

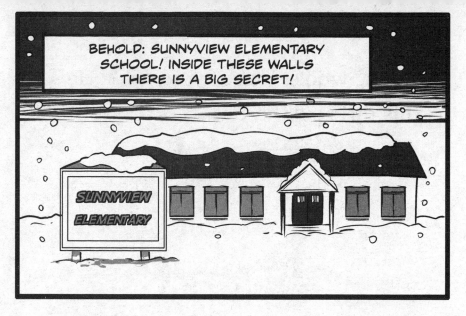

SUNNYVIEW ELEMENTARY

But for now it was perfectly quiet at Sunnyview Elementary. No kids running down the halls, no teachers giving out pop quizzes, no second-grade students reaching into Turbo's cage—

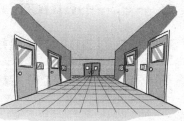

Oh, who's Turbo, you ask? He's this little guy here.

If you couldn't guess, Turbo is a hamster. His fur is mostly white, but he has a big brown spot on his back. He has little pink ears and buck teeth.

And this—er—palace is Turbo's home. Here in the corner of Ms. Beasley's second-grade class.

Turbo, you see, is the official pet
of Sunnyview Elementary's Classroom C.

And even on a day like today,
when the school was closed for
snow, Turbo took his job as classroom pet very seriously.

He made sure to do all his regular
classroom pet things.

He drank some water. *GLUG, GLUG, GLUG.*

He ate some pellets. *MUNCH, MUNCH, MUNCH.*

And he ran on his hamster wheel. *SQUEAK, SQUEAK, SQUEAK.*

When he was finished, only a few

minutes had passed. Now what?
Usually Turbo liked when the kids
went out to recess and he got some
peace and quiet. But today it was
almost *too* quiet.

Suddenly, it wasn't quiet any-
more. Turbo was sure he heard a
rustling coming from the cubbies.

Straining his tiny ears, Turbo listened as hard as he could.

"There is definitely something
there," Turbo said to no one in
particular. "I'm the official pet of
Classroom C, and so it is my duty
to find out the source of this mys-
tery sound!"

Finally, Turbo got to where the noise seemed to be coming from. And then he saw a tail and it belonged to a totally terrible, awful, frightening . . .

THE MOST TERRIBLE, AWFUL, FRIGHTENING CREATURE

Turbo steadied himself and . . .

"Be careful!" yelled the owner of the tail that surely belonged to the most terrible, awful, frightening creature anyone had ever imagined. "If you grab my tail like that, it might break off!"

The strange new visitor turned

to face Turbo. Now that Turbo could get a good look at him, this stranger wasn't quite the most terrible, awful, frightening creature anyone had ever imagined. Unless the person who imagined him was incredibly afraid of small, green-spotted lizards.

"Who are you?" sputtered Turbo.

"I'm Leo," said the small, green-spotted lizard. "I'm from Classroom A. Who are *you*?"

Gasp! Another classroom pet?!

Turbo had always wondered if there were others like him out

there. Turbo stared suspiciously at Leo. Should he reveal his real name?

"What are you doing here in Classroom C?" Turbo decided to ask first.

"I'm here looking for Angelina," replied Leo. "Have you seen her?"

Turbo rubbed his chin. "I don't think so. What does she look like?"

"Well, she's all fuzzy, just like you. And she's got little pink ears, just like you. And she has buck teeth, just like you. Wait . . . are *you* Angelina?"

"Of course not! My name is Turbo," said Turbo. *Oh no!* He had accidentally revealed his real name!

"Oh, well," said Leo, "it didn't hurt to ask. All you fuzzy guys look the same to me."

Suddenly another rustling sound came from the reading nook. Turbo closed his eyes and listened while Leo pulled on a mysterious mask.

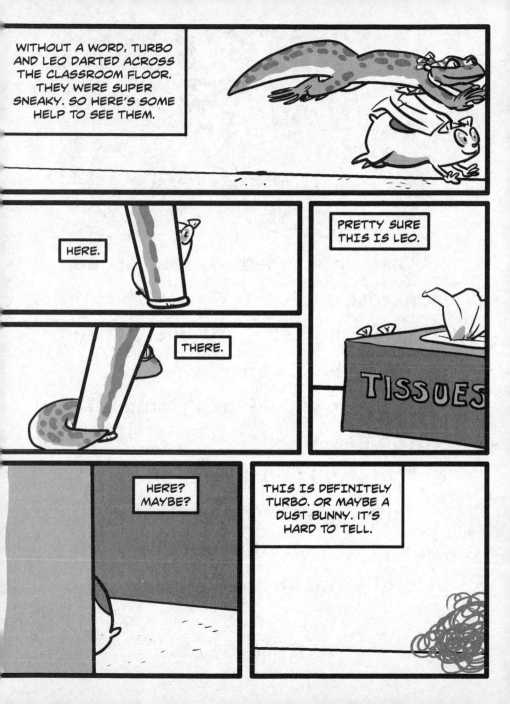

The two stopped in front of the bookcase.

"Nice moves!" Leo said. "They were really . . . *super*."

"Uh, are you wearing a mask?" Turbo asked.

"No," said Leo. "Don't be silly."

Turbo wasn't being silly and he was pretty sure he had seen Leo actually run *up* some *walls*.

Then, on the bookcase, a book
lurched out several inches from the
shelf. A mysterious figure came into
view. It was fuzzy. It had pink ears.
It had buck teeth.

TURBO GETS A SUPER SURPRISE

"Angelina!" cried Leo as he pulled off his mask.

Ah, so this was Angelina. Turbo wondered what she was doing in Classroom C when she said, "Can you help me get this book? I'm tired of all the books in Classroom B. Too many pictures, not enough words."

Another classroom pet?! Turbo was flabbergasted. What a day today was turning out to be!

Angelina started pushing the book farther toward the edge of the shelf. Quick as lightning, Leo raced up the bookcase to help her.

Meanwhile, Turbo ran off to get a pillow to catch the book.

On the count of three, Angelina and Leo gave a big shove, and the book fell right onto the pillow.

Leo skittered down the side of the bookcase, and Angelina simply jumped off the shelf onto the pillow. Now that she was up close, Turbo could see the resemblance.

Turbo shook his head. "I have to admit, I never knew there were any other classroom pets," he said, sort of embarrassed.

"Every classroom has its own pet," explained Angelina. She held out her hand to shake Turbo's.

Turbo rubbed his hand gingerly. "Wow, you're strong!"

"Of course I'm strong!" she said. "I'm a guinea pig and I have super-pig strength!"

Turbo's mouth fell open. "Super-pig strength?" he asked.

He also noticed that she had a perfect white *W* in the middle of her fur.

"But that's not my real super-power," Angelina added.

Superpower? What was going on? But before Turbo could respond, Leo jumped between them.

"Ha-ha, that's enough, Angelina," Leo said quickly. "Okay, well, we'll be getting along. Turbo, it was nice to meet you—"

Suddenly something fluttered onto the floor.

"Hey?" said Turbo. "Is that a . . . mask?"

Leo swiftly scooped up the mask and hid it behind his back.

But Angelina said, "It's too late now, Leo. He knows."

Leo turned around. Turbo wondered if he was about to run away. But when Leo turned *back* around, he was wearing the mask and a

supercool handkerchief with a giant G on it.

Turbo's eyes practically popped out of his head. Angelina was also now wearing a mask and the *W* on her belly almost seemed to be *glowing*.

AND I'M NOT JUST ANGELINA . . . I'M WONDER PIG!

Turbo looked back and forth between the two pets. "You! Guys! Are! Superheroes?!"

Leo nodded. "But this is top secret information, and you must promise to keep it that way," he told Turbo.

Without a word Turbo raced off. Leo and Angelina just looked at each other.

"I guess that was too much for him," said Angelina.

"Well, we are pretty awesome," said Leo.

Suddenly the caped figure leaped back into view.

Now it was Angelina's and Leo's turn to be surprised.

Leo rubbed his eyes. "Another superhero?! This is *great*! Angelina, leave your book here for now. Let's introduce Super Turbo to the team!"

MEET THE TEAM!

"Team?" asked Turbo.

Angelina smiled. "There aren't just other classroom *pets*," she said. "There are other pet *superheroes*! I'll show you the way."

The three heroes scampered over to the vent by the door of Classroom C. Angelina lifted the grate off the

vent so
that Turbo
and Leo could get
inside. They followed her down
the length of the duct until they
came to another grate.

"Hiya, Clever!" Leo said with a
wave as he stepped out.

In a cage way above them, a

green parakeet looked down. "Hey, Leo! Hey, Angelina! Who's that with you guys?"

"This is Super Turbo" said Angelina. "He's the pet protector of Classroom C!"

Clever unlocked her cage and flew down to them. The animals all followed Angelina through the vents. They came out into another room, filled with beakers, scales, and microscopes.

"This is the science lab. Warren lives here," explained Angelina.

Clever flew up to a glass case.

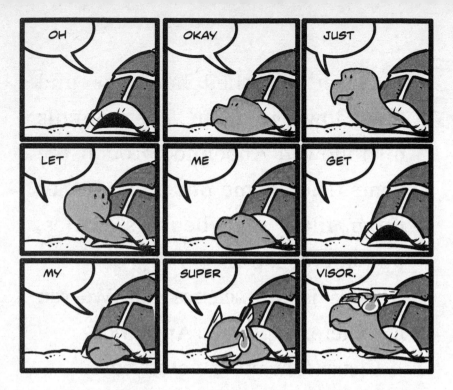

Even with the other animals' help, it still took a very long time to get Warren down to the vents.

"I like your visor," Turbo told Warren.

"Thanks," said Warren. "The . . .

wings . . . make . . . me . . . go . . .
faster."

Leo placed his hands where his
hips would be if geckos indeed had
hips.

SOMETHING SMELLS FISHY

PRINCIPAL

Turbo had never been to the principal's office, but he knew from his time in Classroom C that it was a place to be avoided at all costs. Only students who were in the biggest trouble possible went to the principal's office. So what sort of terrifying pet would live there?! The

vent in the principal's office was
conveniently located right above a
shelf. The room was dark as all the
animals filed out one by one. Turbo
noticed a big cage that was made of
wire—like his—and wood.

Suddenly the lights flickered on.

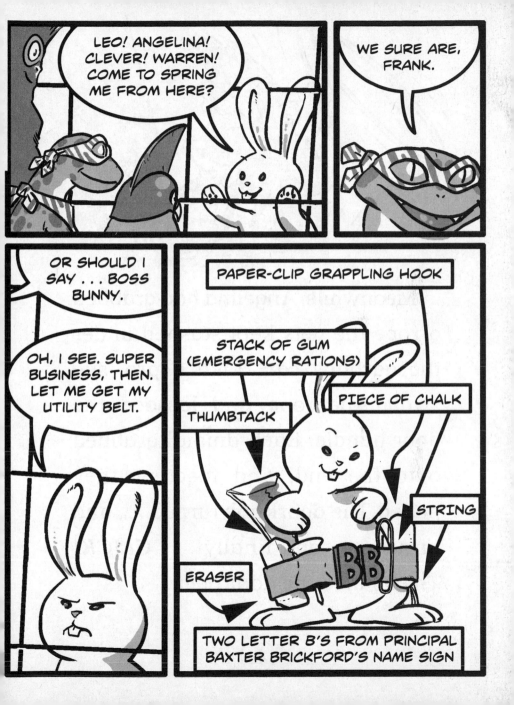

Meanwhile, Angelina had grabbed a rope the pets kept stashed under the garbage can. Like a pro, she swung the rope and lassoed the door handle. Each animal grabbed onto the end, and together they pulled. The doorknob turned . . . and turned . . . and finally . . . CLICK! They pulled the door open.

"Wow!" Turbo exclaimed. He was very impressed.

The animals filed out of the principal's office and into the hallway. Suddenly there was a voice.

But how?

The pets all thought hard.

"I could build a teleporting machine," offered up Warren. "We could teleport Nell out of the fish tank!"

"You can do that?" asked Turbo, shocked.

"Well . . . I never have before," admitted Warren. "But I could try."

"Even if we could teleport Nell down here, she would still need water to breathe," Leo pointed out.

"I have an idea! Wonder Pig, come with me!" Turbo pulled his cape tight and scampered down the hall.

Angelina looked to the others, shrugged,

and ran off after him. The other animals stood around, unsure of what to do.

"So what did you do to end up here in the hallway, Nell?" asked Clever.

Nell flapped a fin, revealing a long, lightning bolt–shaped scar on her side. "It's a long story," she said. "A story for another time."

Just then, everyone stopped talking. A rumbling sound was coming down the hallway. Suddenly Super Turbo came into view. He was rolling along at superspeed in his hamster ball. Wonder Pig was running to catch up with him.

Clever and Frank barely leaped out of the way as Turbo raced toward them, coming to an abrupt stop as he bounced off Warren's hard shell.

Dizzily, Turbo hopped out of the Turbomobile. "We can fill my Turbo-mobile with water, and Nell can ride along with us!"

Leo climbed down the wall he had scurried up. "I don't want to rain on your parade, Super Turbo, but there are holes in that hamster ball. The water will leak out."

"Yeah, but Boss Bunny, you have gum on your utility belt, right? We can chew it up and plug the holes," said Turbo.

Frank rubbed his whiskers. "That sounds almost crazy enough to work."

Clever turned to Nell. "Nell, what do you think?"

Nell looked around at the other fish in her tank, then back at Turbo. "I like this guy! He's nuts! Let's do it!"

Working together, the animal superheroes put Super Turbo's plan into action. The classroom pets with buck teeth—and a lot of the animals had them—chewed up the gum. Clever used her beak to stick the chewed-up gum into every

hole. Warren noticed a bottle cap
on the ground and calculated that
it would take approximately 15.37
bottle caps of water to fill the Turbomobile. Leo scampered up the tank

and back down, carefully filling the bottle cap and then dumping the water into the Turbomobile.

Finally, the job was done. While the superpets held the ball steady, Nell leaped out of her tank and did a perfect triple somersault dive into the Turbomobile.

"Fantastic!" Leo clapped.

"Fantastic Fish! That can be your superhero name!" said Turbo excitedly.

"I like it!" said Nell as she swished her tail. "I'm not just Nell . . . I'm Fantastic Fish!"

SOMETHING *ELSE* SMELLS EVIL

They were all there. Super Turbo,
Wonder Pig, the Great Gecko, the
Green Winger, Professor Turtle,
Boss Bunny, and Fantastic Fish.
And they were ready to fight evil!

The only problem was ... what evil?
The animals looked at one another,
all clearly thinking the same thing.

"So . . . ," began Super Turbo.

"Um . . . ," said the Green Winger.

"Well, uh . . . ," added Boss Bunny.

"I'm hungry," said Professor Turtle.

"Great idea!" exclaimed the Great Gecko. "A snack! We're going to need fuel if we're planning to fight evil today."

The rest of the pets eagerly agreed. Then they crawled, scampered, hopped, flew, rolled, and otherwise walked through the doors of the empty Sunnyview Elementary cafeteria.

"Hold it!" Boss Bunny yelled. "I smell something rotten in here."

"Something rotten? Well, the school *is* closed because of the snow," the Great Gecko offered up. "Maybe they didn't have a chance to take out the trash."

Boss Bunny's pink nose twitched. "This isn't rotten garbage. This is a different smell."

"I don't smell anything," said Fantastic Fish. Although, to be fair, she was underwater.

"Yeah, Boss Bunny, how do you know what evil smells like?" asked Professor Turtle.

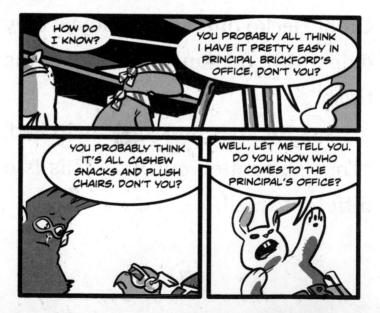

Suddenly Wonder Pig burst out laughing. "Boss Bunny, I'm pretty sure you're just hungry. We all are!"

The Great Gecko nodded. "Keep that nose to the ground,"he told Boss Bunny. "I'm getting a snack!"

The other classroom pets ran off to the pantry, but Super Turbo hung back. Boss Bunny had seemed so sure there was evil afoot, but where? Who? WHAT? Turbo did one last scan of the cafeteria, then ran off to join his new pals.

By the time Super Turbo reached the other classroom pets, the pantry door was already open. The Great Gecko had scurried up the shelves, where he and the Green Winger threw snacks down to the others.

While everyone happily munched on chips, bagels, and crackers shaped oddly like Nell, Super Turbo noticed that Boss Bunny was still standing back, looking troubled. His nose was twitching more than ever. Super Turbo was starting to get the feeling that Boss Bunny was right. And that's when he saw it . . .

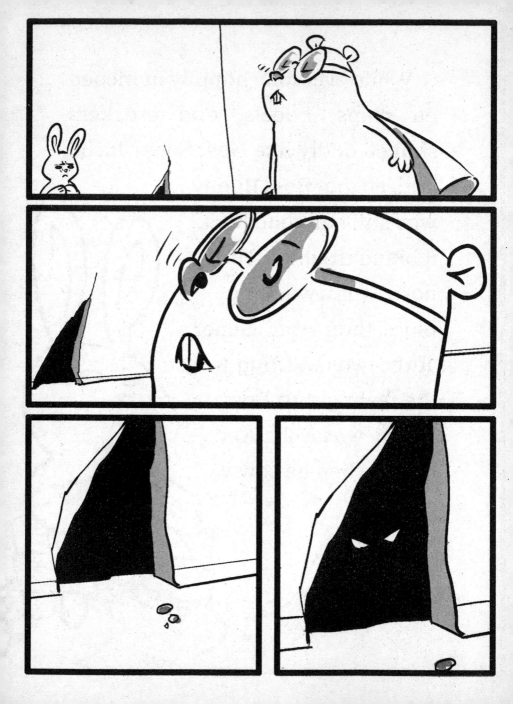

7

WHISKERFACE

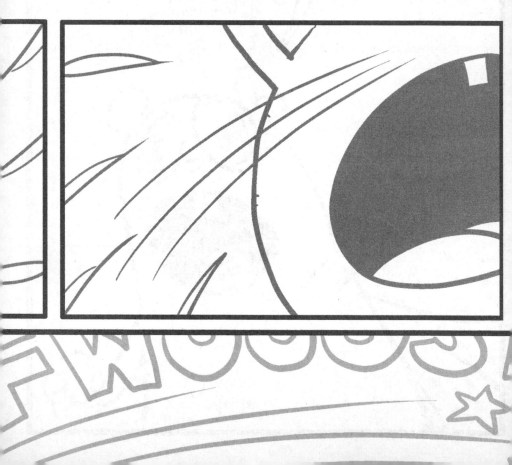

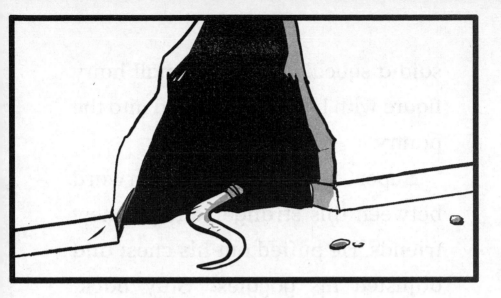

A thin pink tail was sticking out of a hole in the wall.

It certainly has been a day for weird tails, Super Turbo thought.

Suddenly the tail disappeared. In its place a pair of beady yellow eyes stared out.

"Well, well, what do we have here?"

said a squeaky voice. A small hairy figure with big ears marched into the pantry.

Super Turbo stepped forward between this stranger and his new friends. He puffed out his chest and adjusted his goggles. "Stay back, Mr., uh . . . ," he paused, not sure what to call this creature.

"Whiskerface!" yelled the stranger.

"Mr. Whiskerface?" asked Turbo.

"I've been waiting for you all to arrive," Whiskerface said, sinisterly twirling his long whiskers. "You see, with all the classroom pets in one place, I can capture you and take over the school!" Whiskerface laughed a horrible, high-pitched laugh.

Before the super animals could
respond, Whiskerface cried: "But
wait! There's more! Because after
I take over Sunnyview Elementary, I will use the school as my
base . . . to take over the entire
world!"

The pets blinked.

"I think you may have left out a few steps in that plan of yours," said Fantastic Fish.

"Enough distractions!" Whisker-face yelled. "The point is, I have you all where I want you. And now I will make you my prisoners!"

"Oh yeah?" said Wonder Pig, stepping forward. The *W* on her belly once again seemed to be *glowing.* "Well, look around. There's *one* of you and *seven* of us!"

Whiskerface gave a sly grin. "RAT PACK!" he suddenly commanded.

THE PLAN TO TAKE OVER THE WORLD

Through the hole in the wall, a stream of hairy, whiskered, big-eared creatures came pouring into the pantry. In seconds Super Turbo and the other classroom pets were surrounded. Super Turbo tightened his cape. This was it.

In seconds the entire pantry was consumed in an epic battle of good versus evil. Wonder Pig got behind Fantastic Fish and launched the Turbomobile forward. It rolled on a perfect path, scattering Rat Pack- ers like bowling pins. The Great

Gecko scampered back up on the
table, where he and the Green
Winger pelted the rats with grapes
and ketchup packets. Boss Bunny
climbed atop Professor
Turtle's shell and

fought off the Rat Packers with his
eraser.

In the chaos Super Turbo saw an
opening. He launched himself at
Whiskerface and tackled the very

mouse-looking rat off of the bagel
he was standing on. The two of them
rolled around on the floor. Super
Turbo's goggles were fogging up,
and it was hard to see. When they
cleared, he saw that Whiskerface

had been stuffed *into* the bagel during the battle. And the evil rat was now wearing it like a tutu!

But at the same time, the tide had turned against the classroom pets. A group of Rat Packers was rolling the Turbomobile back and forth. Inside the bubble, Fantastic Fish looked like she was seasick.

Professor Turtle had retreated inside his own shell, and a couple of

laughing Rat Packers were playing catch with his visor.

Boss Bunny had been tied up with the string from his own utility belt.

A swarm of Rat Packers had cornered the Green Winger and prevented her from flying.

The Great Gecko had almost escaped by running up a wall, but a Rat Packer got lucky and caught the tip of his tail.

Even Wonder Pig, with her super-pig strength, was captured and down for the count.

Super Turbo suddenly realized that he was the only classroom pet left standing. The fate of his new friends, his school, and perhaps the entire WORLD depended on him!

WHEN HAMSTERS FLY!

Super Turbo had to come up with a plan. And fast! He scanned the pantry. The Rat Pack was distracted trying to keep his new friends from escaping. Meanwhile, Whiskerface *was* escaping. And that's when Super Turbo saw it.

Now, you know that a hamster

cannot fly. Maybe if you put a hamster in a catapult or something, you could call that flying. But that's not very nice. But on this day, against these enemies, well . . . guess what? Super Turbo flew!

With a thud, Super Turbo landed atop the table in the pantry. How long before the Rat Pack noticed him? The answer was . . . not long. Already they were racing after him.

Suddenly a lightbulb went on over Super Turbo's head. Well, it didn't go on, but it was there. And there was a long string hanging from it.

Super Turbo took a deep breath. He adjusted his goggles. He fluffed up his cape. And then with all the hamster speed he could muster, he ran as fast as he could to the edge of the table, leaped into the air, and

caught the string that hung from the
lightbulb.

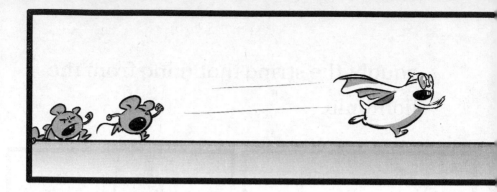

KLANGALANGALANG!

The sound was unbearably loud.
Especially if you happened to be

a tiny little rodent with giant ears. Everyone knows rats hate loud noises! The evil Rat Packers fell down, clutching their ears.

Whiskerface, who was trapped in the bagel tutu, ordered his Rat Pack to cover his ears. But because of the fire alarm, the Rat Pack couldn't hear him. Instead they started crawling back through the hole in the wall. Seeing that he was deserted, Whiskerface turned and ran as well.

As he did, Super Turbo was pretty sure he heard Whiskerface yell, "I'll get you, Super Turbo! This isn't the last you'll see of me!"

THE SUPERPET SUPERHERO LEAGUE!

Later on, in the reading nook in the corner of Classroom C, the new friends gathered to talk about their exciting day.

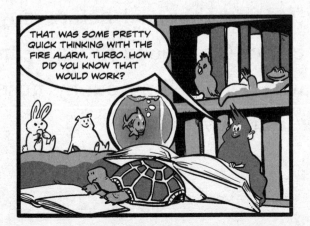

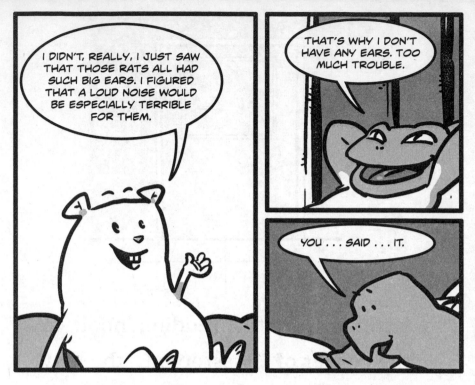

Angelina turned to Frank. "And I have to say, Frank, you definitely sniffed out that evil before any of us could. It's a good thing we have your super-smelling bunny nose to use from now on."

"Sunnyview is in good hands, thanks to us," said Warren, proudly.

All the pets smiled, content with themselves. All the pets but Leo. He frowned.

114

WHAT'S WRONG, LEO?
WELL, NELL, WE DID A GOOD JOB TODAY. WE SAVED THE SCHOOL!
WE MAYBE EVEN SAVED THE WHOLE WORLD!
I STILL THINK THERE WERE A FEW STEPS MISSING FROM THAT PLAN.

"Super!" shouted Clever.

"Pet!" yelled Nell.

"Superhero League!" cried Frank.

"And I propose that Classroom C, right here, be our meeting place," added Angelina.

All the animals agreed it was the perfect place for a team of superhero pets.

o   o   o

That night, Turbo returned to his comfy cage in the corner of Classroom C. He carefully folded up his Super Turbo gear and returned it to his secret hiding spot. He looked at

116

his hamster wheel, his hamster pellets, his water bottle.

Tomorrow, school would be back
in session. For all the students, all
the teachers, and even Principal
Brickford, it would be no different
from any other day. But it *would* be
different. Because tomorrow, and
forever after, Sunnyview Elementary was under the protection of . . .

Normally, Sunnyview Elementary was filled with kids and teachers and all the things that make up a school. But it was after hours. Everyone was at home or asleep. And not a creature was stirring, except for a—what is that? A mouse?

"Fellow rats!" a small, fuzzy creature with huge ears and long whiskers addressed a crowd of other creatures just like him. Although he was a bit smaller than the rest, his whiskers were longer. This is why he was called. . . Whiskerface!

"I suppose you're all wondering why I called you here tonight!" he continued.

There was a chorus of whispers. "Uh, was today Taco Tuesday?" asked a tiny voice from the back.

"No!" roared back Whiskerface. "It's not even Tuesday, it's Friday!"

"As you all know, the Rat Pack recently suffered a defeat at the paws of the Pampered Pets of Sunnyview Elementary."

Whiskerface stroked his whiskers as he reminded his Rat Pack what had happened.

A team of classroom pets had showed up in his cafeteria and halted his plan to take over Sunnyview Elementary and, eventually, the world!

"But as your fearless leader, I have taken steps to make sure that the Rat Pack will never be defeated again!" Whiskerface cried.